THE Coal THIEF

Written by **Alane Adams**
Illustrated by **Lauren Gallegos**

RODINA
PRESS

Rodina Press
158 N. Glassell St. Suite 202
Orange, CA 92866
www.rodinapress.com

Printed in the United States of America

Library of Congress Cataloging-in-Publication Data
Adams, Alane.
The Coal Thief / Alane Adams; Illustrated by Lauren Gallegos. — 1st ed.
p. cm.
ISBN 978-0-9862436-0-8
2014921055

First Edition
10 9 8 7 6 5 4 3 2 1

Book design by Lauren Gallegos

To my father, the original coal thief. —A. A.

In memory of Grandpa Gale, who loved trains. —L. G.

Girard, Pennsylvania, 1929

One morning, Georgie went into the kitchen. He poked around the potbellied stove, hoping to find a stray lump of coal.

"Don't bother, Georgie," Mama said, "there's been no coal for three days."

"But I'm cold." He shivered in the icy kitchen.

"Put your coat on."

Georgie took his coat down from the hook. "When's Papa coming home?"

"He's fixing a broken rail line. He should be home for supper."

Just then the door burst open, and his friend
Harley rushed in.

"Grab your boots, Georgie. We're going on
an adventure."

Georgie hurried to put on his boots.
"Where are we going?"

"Train's coming."

"Aw, Harley, trains come every day."

"Not this train. Come on, we don't want to miss it."

Harley had a wheelbarrow out front.
They started walking down the road.

Georgie had a lot of questions. "What's the wheelbarrow for?" he asked.

"It's a surprise. This train's carrying something special."

Georgie's heart beat faster. "Where's it coming from?"

"Virginia."

Georgie frowned. "What's in Virginia?"

"Black gold. Hurry up. We don't have much time."

Georgie trotted to keep up with Harley.
They walked to the train depot at the
edge of town.

"Is this where the black gold is?"
Georgie asked.

"Quiet, we don't want anyone to see us."

"Why not?" he whispered.

"It'll spoil the surprise."

Harley crouched down behind a
locomotive, so Georgie did the same.
It was cold. Georgie's toes stuck out
of the holes in his boots.

The blast of a whistle made him jump.

"Here she comes!" Harley cried.

A steam engine pulled into the station.

Harley jumped up. "This way, Georgie."

They ran along the tracks to the end
of the train.

Harley lifted him up the side of a railcar.
Georgie looked inside.

It was filled with chunks of coal.
An entire mountain of it.

Black gold.

Georgie looked down at Harley. "What should I do?"

"Climb inside and toss some over."

Georgie blinked. "Isn't that stealing?"

Harley scowled at him. "Ain't you tired of being cold every morning?"

"Yes, but—"

"Don't be a chicken, Georgie, or I'll tell on you and say it was your idea."

Georgie slowly climbed over the top and landed on the hard lumps. He picked one up and tossed it over.

Harley caught it and set it on the ground. "Another," he said.

Georgie grabbed two lumps and dropped them down.

Harley grinned up at him. "It's gonna be a long winter, Georgie. Keep it coming."

Georgie began throwing the pieces faster and faster.
Suddenly the train gave a jerk. Georgie fell backward.
"Georgie, get out of there!" Harley called.
But the mountain of coal had swallowed him up.

The train began to pick up speed.
"Help me, Harley!" Georgie shouted.
He tried to push off the coal, but he just
sank deeper into the pile.

Then Papa's head appeared over the top of the railcar.

"Time to go, Georgie." Papa reached out his hand and pulled Georgie free. They sat on the edge of the railcar. When Papa said jump, Georgie jumped.

Papa helped Georgie to his feet. "If I hadn't seen you boys head this way, you'd be halfway to Texas by now."

Georgie craned his neck, looking for Harley, but his friend had turned tail and run. "Sorry, Papa."

"You know stealing's wrong?" Papa said sternly.

Georgie nodded, feeling the shame curl his toes.

They walked back to the little mountain of coal.

Papa scratched his head. "Train's gone now. We can't give back the coal. But I've got an idea what to do with it. Help me load it."

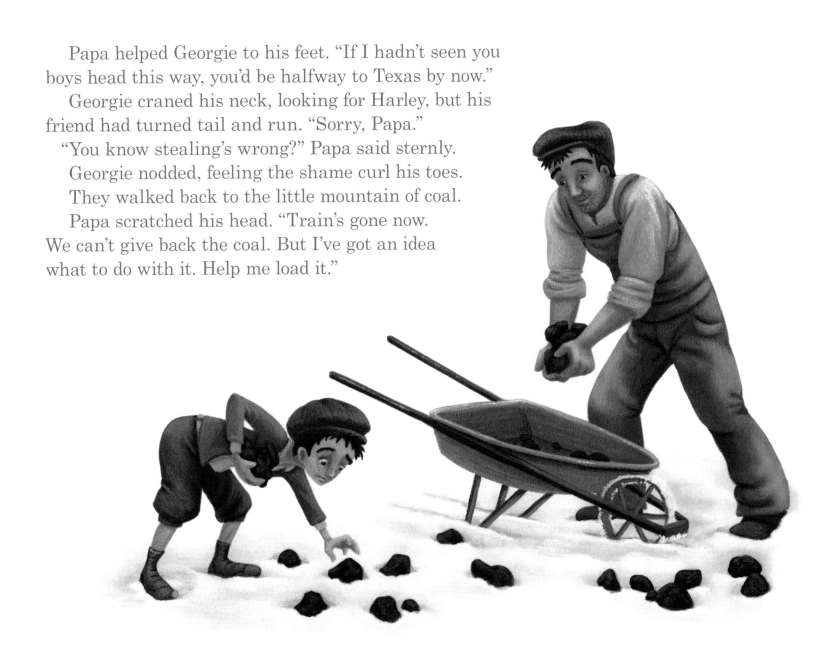

They rolled the wheelbarrow down the street to a house with a sagging front porch. "This is Widow Kolbach's house," Georgie said.

Papa handed him two large chunks of coal. "Leave this by her door. Then knock twice and run on back here."

Georgie climbed the steps. The porch creaked under his weight. Dropping the coal, Georgie rapped his knuckles on the door and ran back to Papa. They hid behind some bushes.

After a moment, Mrs. Kolbach opened the door. When she spied the coal, she lifted it up, holding it to her chest and cried, "God bless you!"

Georgie's heart felt so warm it sent tingles right down to his toes. "Who else, Papa?"

"Come on, the Children's Home is just down the road."

They trundled the cart to a large brick house. Kids ran about in the yard. One of the boys came over to the fence. Georgie piled chunks of coal in his arms.

"Thank you," the boy said. "We've been freezing all winter." He shivered in the thin shirt he wore.

Georgie hesitated, then took off his coat.
"Here, take this. It's too small for me anyway."
The boy's eyes grew wide. "You mean it?"
Georgie nodded, piling the coat on top of
the boy's arms.

Papa had many more stops to make. By the time they got home, Georgie was covered in coal dust from elbow to ears, and there was only one chunk of coal left.

"Who are we giving this last piece to?"

"That's for your mother," Papa winked. "Maybe she won't notice you gave away your good coat."

They reached the porch. Georgie climbed the steps, but Papa turned to go.

"Aren't you coming in, Papa?"

"I still have a day's work to do, son. Run along now."

Georgie hesitated. Then he ran down the steps and threw his arms around Papa's waist.

"I love you, Papa."

Papa patted Georgie on the head. "I love you, too, little coal thief."